This book belongs to

For my husband, Jerome,
and my father, Konrad.
With all my love.

Sky Pony Press books may be purchased in bulk at special discounts for sales promotion, corporate gifts, fund-raising, or educational purposes. Special editions can also be created to specifications. For details, contact the Special Sales Department, Sky Pony Press, 307 West 36th Street, 11th Floor, New York, NY 10018 or info@skyhorsepublishing.com.

Sky Pony® is a registered trademark of Skyhorse Publishing, Inc.®, a Delaware corporation.

Visit our website at www.skyponypress.com.

10 9 8 7 6 5 4 3 2 1

Manufactured in China, April 2018
This product conforms to CPSIA 2008

Library of Congress Cataloging-in-Publication Data

Names: Krebs, Chrissie, author, illustrator.
Title: This is a circle / Chrissie Krebs.
Description: First Sky Pony edition. | New York : Skyhorse Publishing, 2018.
| "First published by Random House Australia in 2016." | Summary:
Illustrations and simple, rhyming text introduce circles and squares as a
most unusual group of animals sings, sails, huffs, and puffs.
Identifiers: LCCN 2018007510 | ISBN 9781510731288 (hc)
Subjects: | CYAC: Stories in rhyme. | Animals--Fiction. | Circle--Fiction. |
Square--Fiction. | Humorous stories.
Classification: LCC PZ8.3.K8668 Thi 2018 | DDC [E]--dc23 LC record available at https://lccn.loc.gov/2018007510

Cover design by Kate Gartner
Cover illustration by Hannah Janzen

Print ISBN: 978-1-5107-3128-8
E-Book ISBN: 978-1-5107-3129-5

THIS IS A CIRCLE

Chrissie Krebs

Sky Pony Press

New York

This is a
circle.

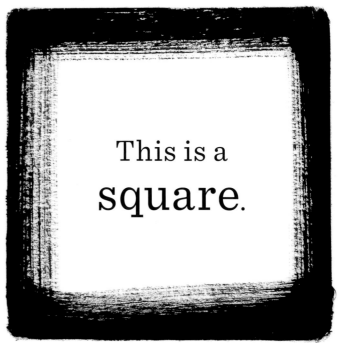

This is a
square.

This is a wild-looking one-eyed bear.

This is a **ball**.

This is a **box**.

This is a pant-wearing fluffy-eared fox.

This is a **scarf**

plus a **hat**,

a **car**

and **boat**,

a song-singing cat

and

a tap-dancing goat.

The goat climbs the box
while wearing the hat,
which frightens the fox
and angers the cat.

The **bear** sails the **boat**
while the **cat** drives the **car**
around that white **goat**
who looks on from afar.

The **fox** doesn't care for this silly stuff,

so he sits on the **square** in a bit of a huff.

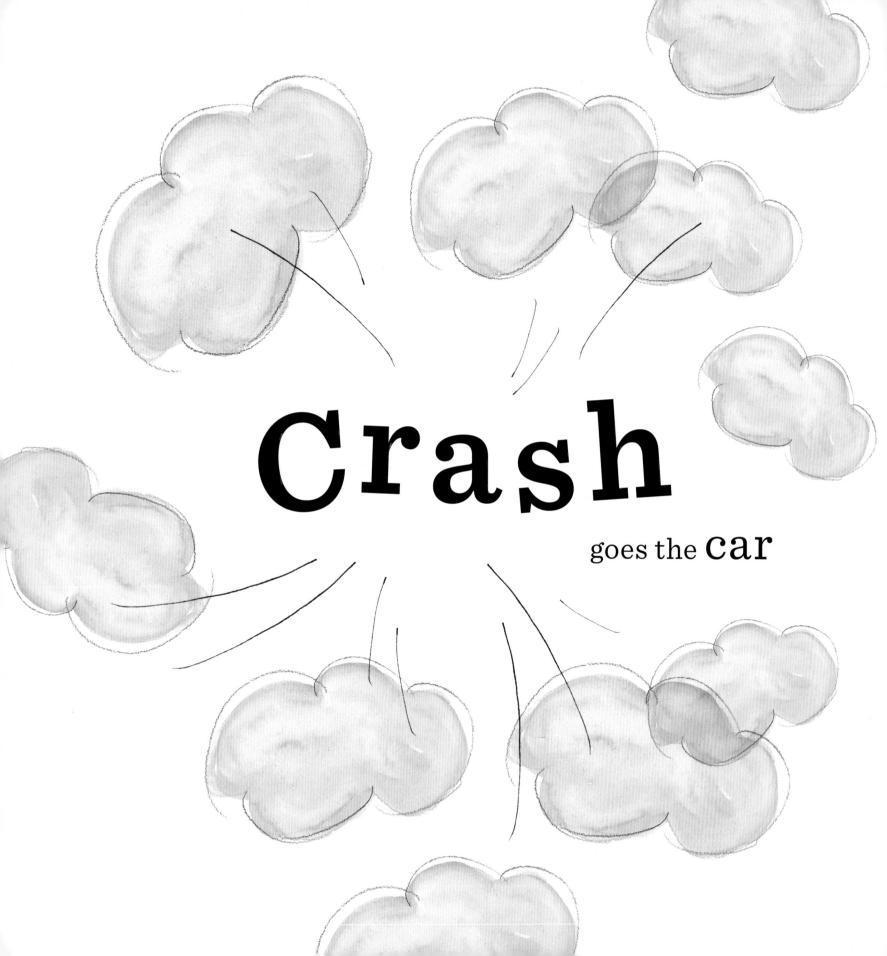

Crash

goes the car

and up flies the cat
to the top of the box
with the goat in the hat.

The **cat** sings a song

as the **goat** does a dance,

while the **bear** sails along

past the **fox** wearing pants.

The **fox** throws the **ball** at the big old bear's head,

which makes
bear see stars

but then
he sees **red!**

The angry **bear** chases the pant-wearing fox

in rather large circles around that big **box**.

The fox runs so fast
that he puffs out the bear.
Fox climbs the box
as if running on air!

Now the fox and the cat
and the tap-dancing goat
all look down low
at the bear and the boat.

The bear gets so mad at being

stuck on the ground

that he starts to stack all the

things lying around.

The car, the boat,

the scarf, ball and square

pile on top of each other,

then up climbs the bear.

And finally the **bear** is on top of the box

with the **cat** and the **goat**
and the pant-wearing **fox**.

They stare at each other
and then start to frown.

Now they are **up** here . . .

How do they get down?